SCOOBY-DOO!

THE SECRET OF THE FLYING SAUCER

Stone Arch Books
A Capstone Imprint

You Choose Stories: Scooby-Doo
is published by Stone Arch Books,
A Capstone Imprint
1710 Roe Crest Drive
North Mankato, Minnesota 56003
www.capstonepub.com

CAPS33979

Cataloging-in-Publication Data is available on the
Library of Congress website.
ISBN: 978-1-4965-0478-4 [Library Hardcover]
ISBN: 978-1-4965-0480-7 [Paperback]
ISBN: 978-1-4965-2364-8 [eBook]

Summary: Scooby-Doo and the Mystery Inc. gang
discover a flying saucer in Kansas.

Printed in China.
042015   008866RRDF15

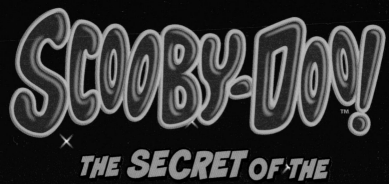

SCOOBY-DOO!

THE SECRET OF THE
FLYING SAUCER

written by
Laurie S. Sutton

illustrated by
Scott Neely

THE MYSTERY INC. GANG!

SCOOBY-DOO

SKILLS: Loyal; super snout
BIO: This happy-go-lucky hound avoids scary situations at all costs, but he'll do anything for a Scooby Snack!

SHAGGY ROGERS

SKILLS: Lucky; healthy appetite
BIO: This laid-back dude would rather look for grub than search for clues, but he usually finds both!

FRED JONES, JR.

SKILLS: Athletic; charming
BIO: The leader and oldest member of the gang. He's a good sport—and good at them, too!

DAPHNE BLAKE

SKILLS: Brains; beauty
BIO: As a sixteen-year-old fashion queen, Daphne solves her mysteries in style.

VELMA DINKLEY

SKILLS: Clever; highly intelligent
BIO: Although she's the youngest member of Mystery Inc., Velma's an old pro at catching crooks.

← YOU CHOOSE →

SCOOBY-DOO!

A mysterious spaceship has landed, but does the alien crew come in peace or are they planning something more sinister? Only YOU can help Scooby-Doo and the Mystery Inc. gang figure out this paranormal puzzle.

Follow the directions at the bottom of each page. The choices YOU make will change the outcome of the story. After you finish one path, go back and read the others for more Scooby-Doo adventures!

YOU CHOOSE the path to solve...

THE SECRET OF THE FLYING SAUCER

"I'm starving!" Shaggy moans as Mystery Inc. drives along a country road in Kansas, right in the heart of the United States.

"Re, too!" Scooby-Doo agrees with his best pal.

GRUUUMBLE! Scooby's stomach agrees, too!

"We'll find a roadside farm stand or diner for you soon," Velma promises.

"Ri want hot dogs!" Scooby says.

"I want barbeque!" Shaggy declares.

"Well, we're in Kansas and the state is known for its BBQ ribs!" Fred says and licks his lips as he drives the Mystery Machine.

Turn the page.

"I can find the nearest restaurant on my phone," Velma says. She checks her smartphone. "*Hmmm*. I'm not getting a signal."

"Don't worry. I've made a few upgrades to our GPS system. I can find out where the nearest town is," Fred declares confidently. He presses a few buttons on the control panel.

All of the members of Mystery Inc. watch the GPS monitor display. Nothing happens.

"Like, are we there yet?" Shaggy wonders hopefully.

"Well that can't be right," Fred observes as he stares at the blank screen. "The GPS is acting . . . strange."

Suddenly the engine of the Mystery Machine sputters and coasts to a stop. Fred tries to restart the vehicle. It makes a few sad sounds but won't start.

"Oh, no! Like, this is exactly what happened to the Mystery Machine in New Orleans just before our last adventure," Shaggy says.

"Relax, Shaggy. We're in the middle of Kansas. What could happen?" Daphne reassures her friends.

ZOOOOOMMM!

Something flies over the Mystery Machine at very high speed and very low height!

"Zoinks! What was that?" Shaggy shrieks. He grabs Scooby and hugs his best pal.

"I think it was a crop-duster plane," Fred says.

"It was going too fast to be a crop duster," Velma declares.

CRAAAAAASSHHH!

"Whatever it was, it just crashed in that cornfield!" Daphne says.

"Someone might be in trouble and need our help," Fred decides. "Let's go!"

The Mystery Inc. gang jumps out of the van and runs into the cornfield.

Turn the page.

Fred, Velma, and Daphne lead the way through the rows of tall cornstalks. Shaggy and Scooby struggle to keep up with their friends.

"Like, this corn is so tall that I can't see where I'm going. A person could get lost in here," Shaggy says.

"Rand a dog, too," Scooby-Doo points out.

At last Shaggy and Scooby catch up to the rest of their pals. They are standing as still as statues.

"Don't move!" Fred warns.

Then Shaggy and Scooby-Doo see what their friends see!

There is a big circle of flattened cornstalks in the middle of the giant field. In the center of the circle is what looks like . . .

"A flying saucer!" Shaggy gasps.

"Ruh-roh," Scooby gulps.

"Look! Somebody . . . or something . . . is coming out!" Daphne exclaims.

The pals watch as a hatch opens in the side of the saucer. A stairway folds out and a small gray creature exits the vehicle. He is very thin and has a big head and large black eyes. The strange figure thumps the hull of the ship with his fist.

"Ha! I try that with the Mystery Machine all the time. It never works," Fred says.

"I don't think that's what he's doing," Velma says.

A small service hatch opens where the little gray creature hit the hull. A rainbow of light flows out of the opening.

"That's a control panel," Velma says. "It must have been damaged in the crash."

"How do you know that?" Daphne asks.

"I can see it with my glasses. I can see everything with my glasses," Velma replies.

"Zoinks! Is this an alien invasion?" Shaggy worries. "What should we do?"

If Mystery Inc. runs and contacts the authorities, turn to page 12.

If the gang investigates some more, turn to page 14.

If they get abducted by aliens, turn to page 16.

The kids of Mystery Inc. trudge into the nearest town and look for a sheriff or police officer to tell about the saucer.

At last they see a small police station. They go inside and find a sheriff and a deputy working at their desks.

"A flying saucer just crashed in a cornfield!" Fred blurts.

The sheriff does not even look up from her paperwork.

"There's no such thing as flying saucers," she declares.

"But we saw . . ." Velma begins.

"I don't care what you *think* you saw. I hear enough of that UFO nonsense from my deputy," the sheriff says. "Now beat it."

The gang is disappointed. They leave the small office and walk down the street.

"Hey, kids! The sheriff doesn't believe you, but I do!" the deputy says as he trots after them. "Show me the crash site."

The gang gets into the deputy's squad car and they drive away. No one sees the sheriff watching them. She makes a secret phone call.

Mystery Inc. guides the deputy to where the Mystery Machine is parked on the side of the country road. Before they head into the cornfield the deputy pulls out special gear that is designed to find UFOs.

"You won't need any of that. The saucer is in plain sight," Velma tells him.

But when they get to the crash site, the saucer is gone!

"Like, where did it go?" Shaggy wonders.

Suddenly Scooby's nose twitches. *SNIFF! SNIFF!* At the same time, the deputy's detector sounds. *BEEP! BEEP!*

If they follow Scooby-Doo's clue, turn to page 18.
If they follow the deputy's clue, turn to page 25.

Mystery Inc. is surprised to see a flying saucer sitting in the middle of an ordinary Kansas cornfield. An alien is walking around outside the ship. As soon as the creature goes back inside the saucer, Fred makes a decision.

"Let's investigate!" Fred says.

"You guys can go ahead without Scooby and me," Shaggy says.

Daphne reaches into her purse and pulls out a handful of treats. "Would you do it for some Scooby Snacks?" she asks.

"Rokay!" Scooby agrees. He gobbles up the snacks.

"Like, what are we waiting for?" Shaggy says as he chomps on the treats.

Shaggy and Scooby follow the rest of the gang up to the flying saucer. Velma inspects the landing gear. Fred thumps on the hull.

"Where's that control panel the alien opened?" Fred wonders.

"Don't bang on the hull! The alien might hear you!" Daphne worries.

Suddenly the saucer starts to rise into the air. The kids back away from the spaceship.

"Help!" Velma yells. "I'm stuck!"

"Ruh-roh!" Scooby gulps and points his paw at Velma. Her sweater is caught on one of the landing struts.

Fred jumps up and grabs Velma's ankle, but he can't pull her loose. He starts to lift off with the saucer, too. Daphne snags Fred's foot with the strap of her purse, but she gets dragged up, too!

"Shaggy! Scooby! Grab on! Your weight will pull us free!" Velma shouts.

Shaggy grabs Daphne's leg. Scooby holds on to Shaggy. The gang dangles like a loose chain from the flying saucer!

Suddenly the landing strut starts to fold into the saucer. Mystery Inc. is pulled into the spaceship as it flies to an unknown destination!

If the saucer lands somewhere on Earth, turn to page 20.
If the saucer lands somewhere underwater, turn to page 27.

The Mystery Inc. gang hides in the cornfield and watches the small gray alien work on the saucer's control panel. They are surprised to see more aliens suddenly run out of the ship. The aliens talk to each other as if excited about something.

"I wonder what's got them so stirred up," Fred says.

One of the aliens points toward Mystery Inc. even though the kids are hidden behind the tall stalks of corn.

"Ruh-roh," Scooby gulps as the aliens start to rush in their direction.

"Run!" Fred shouts.

The gang splits up and runs through the cornfield. Shaggy and Scooby split left. Daphne and Velma split right. Fred heads back toward the Mystery Machine. He spots a tractor parked in the middle of the corn rows. Fred climbs on board and starts its engine. *PUTT-PUTT-PUTT.* The engine isn't very powerful. The aliens catch up to Fred!

Fred tries to escape the aliens by driving the tractor through the cornfield. The tractor is too slow! The aliens jump up onto the tractor and grab Fred. He turns the steering wheel and tries to shake off the aliens. The tractor bounces over the plowed furrows like it's going over speed bumps.

"Oof! Ouch!" Fred yelps.

One of the aliens falls off the tractor, but the other one hangs on to Fred. He zaps Fred with a ray gun. *ZAAAT!* Fred is hit with a jolt of energy. His hair stands on end and his limbs freeze. He falls off the tractor.

I hope the rest of the gang gets away, Fred thinks as he lies helpless on the ground.

If the aliens go after **Shaggy** and **Scooby,** turn to page **23.**
If the aliens chase **Daphne** and **Velma,** turn to page **29.**

Scooby puts his nose to the ground and trots to the center of the empty corn circle.

"Something made this crop circle," the deputy says.

"This is where we saw the saucer," Fred tells him. "It crushed the cornstalks."

"But where is it now?" Daphne wonders.

"Rover rere!" Scooby shouts. He holds up a half-eaten sandwich.

"Like, I didn't know that aliens ate Earth food," Shaggy says.

Scooby starts to dig at the dirt. He reveals a metal structure under the soil.

"It's a hatch!" Velma gasps.

"I'll bet that saucer went underground," Fred says. "But, how do *we* get down there?"

"Rover rere!" Scooby says. He poses like a bird dog pointing at a spot on the ground.

"Let's follow that sandwich," says Velma.

The deputy and Mystery Inc. find a metal trapdoor hidden under the flattened cornstalks. It opens easily and they climb down a ladder into the dark. Shaggy and Scooby start to shiver.

"Like, flying saucers and aliens are scary in the daylight, but they're even scarier in the dark," Shaggy moans.

They reach the bottom of the ladder and stand in a tiny space with no door. Daphne takes a flashlight out of her purse.

"This looks like a dead end," Daphne says as she swings the light around.

"Zoinks! Don't say *dead*, Daphne!" Shaggy whimpers.

"I hate to say it, but I think our investigation is over before it's even started," Fred sighs.

"Good! Let's get out of here!" Shaggy says.

"Rhat about the rummy randwich?" Scooby asks.

If the gang climbs back up the ladder, turn to page 32.
If they continue to look for a door, turn to page 48.

Scooby-Doo and his pals are trapped inside the landing gear hatch of the flying saucer. They have no idea where they are going. Daphne pulls a flashlight out of her purse and looks around.

"I don't see a way to open the hatch," Daphne says. "We're stuck in here until we land."

"Like, where do you think that will be? It's spooky in here!" Shaggy asks nervously.

"Ri'm hungry," Scooby whimpers as his tummy rumbles.

"Here, have a Scooby Snack," Daphne says and tosses a treat to the cowering canine. Shaggy opens his mouth like a baby bird and Daphne tosses a snack to him, too.

Suddenly the hatch below them starts to open. The landing gear begins to deploy. Mystery Inc. almost falls out of the flying saucer! The gang hangs from the landing strut as the ship drops down toward the roof of a skyscraper.

Turn to page 22.

"Hang on! We're coming in for a landing!" Fred shouts.

The saucer touches down on the roof. The kids jump off the landing strut and run across the roof. They hide behind a large air-conditioning unit and carefully peek back at the saucer.

"Why is an alien saucer landing on the roof of a skyscraper?" Fred wonders aloud. "There's a mystery here!"

The gang watches as the main hatch of the saucer opens and several aliens appear. They cover the ship with a large tarp and then go into the building.

"This is our chance to gather clues and solve the secret of this saucer!" Fred declares.

If Mystery Inc. follows the aliens into the building, turn to page 34.

If the gang investigates inside the saucer, turn to page 52.

Shaggy and Scooby run wildly through the cornfield. They have no idea where they are going. They rush around in circles and almost run into the aliens! The pals grab a few cornstalks and disguise themselves as scarecrows. The aliens race right past them.

"Like, that was a close one, Scoob!" Shaggy sighs in relief.

"Ruh-roh, Rhaggy," Scooby gasps and points a paw at something behind his pal.

Shaggy turns and sees a runaway tractor speeding toward them. A gray alien is trying to steer the machine but is not doing a very good job.

"Zoinks! Run, Scooby-Doo!" Shaggy shrieks.

The tractor follows Shaggy and Scooby down the corn row. The alien can hardly hang on. Suddenly Shaggy trips on an ear of corn and tumbles into Scooby. The two pals get tangled up and roll like a snowball!

Turn the page.

Shaggy and Scooby hit a bump in the ground and bounce high into the air. They come down and land on the tractor with the alien!

Shaggy and the alien stare at each other for a moment. They are so surprised that no one knows what to do. Suddenly Scooby taps Shaggy on the shoulder and points at something ahead of them. The tractor is heading toward the saucer. They are going to crash!

"*Yaaa!*" Shaggy shrieks.

"*Yaaa!*" the alien yells.

Shaggy and the alien grab the tractor's steering wheel at the same time. They twist the wheel in opposite directions. The tractor heads full steam ahead for disaster!

If Shaggy turns the tractor just in time, turn to page 36.
If the tractor crashes into the saucer, turn to page 55.

"This way!" the deputy says and runs into the rows of corn.

He disappears from sight as soon as he enters the tall stalks of corn, but the gang can hear the UFO detector beep faster and faster.

"Come on," Fred says. "There's a mystery here — a mystery of a missing flying saucer!"

The kids hurry into the corn rows. Even though the plowed furrows are straight, the tall stalks and broad leaves of the corn plants make it hard to see where they are going. They are surprised when they bump into the deputy at the edge of a crop circle. They are even more surprised to see a farmhouse sitting in the middle of the circle.

"This wasn't here yesterday," the deputy announces. He points his UFO detector at the structure. *BEEP! BEEP!*

Suddenly the door to the house opens all by itself.

Turn the page.

"Zoinks! It's an alien house!" Shaggy shrieks.

"No, it's a Smart House!" Velma declares. She points out the electronics on the outside of the structure.

Velma runs inside. The rest of the gang and the deputy follow her and find a plain, country-style living room.

"Like, this place doesn't look so smart," Shaggy observes.

A robot the size of a fire hydrant comes out of a wall and zooms up to Shaggy. Another robot appears, and then another and another. They surround Mystery Inc. and the deputy and start to close in on them.

"Quick, everybody. Find a way to turn off the house!" Fred shouts.

The gang splits up. Daphne finds a panel of buttons in the kitchen. Velma and Fred spot a computer screen in the front hall.

If Shaggy and Scooby try to help Daphne, turn to page 68.
If Velma and Fred can't stop the robots, turn to page 86.

Mystery Inc. is trapped inside the saucer. They are all scrunched up in the landing gear hatch with no way out. They can feel that the saucer is flying, but where is it going?

"Like, are we there yet?" Shaggy moans.

"I think we are! Look, the hatch is opening!" Velma says.

"Hang on!" Fred shouts.

The gang hangs on to the strut as the saucer comes in for a landing. As soon as the saucer is on the ground, the gang drops down. Their feet land in something wet and squishy.

"*Ewww,*" Daphne complains.

"It's okay, Daphne, it's just water," Velma explains.

"Where are we?" Fred wonders.

"Well, we're not in Kansas anymore," Velma says and points to the clear dome arching over their heads. On the other side of the dome is the ocean!

Turn the page.

"We're underwater," Fred gasps.

"We're in trouble! Here come the aliens!" Shaggy gulps.

The saucer hatch opens and several gray creatures exit the spaceship. They spot Mystery Inc. and jump in surprise.

"Run!" Fred yelps.

The gang splits up and runs in different directions. Shaggy and Scooby scramble one way. Fred runs another way. Daphne and Velma race off in a third direction.

The aliens are confused. They can't decide who to chase!

If the aliens go after Shaggy and Scooby, turn to page 71.
If the aliens chase Daphne and Velma, turn to page 89.

Daphne and Velma run away from the aliens through the cornfield. They can hear the creatures following them. The two friends come into a clearing in the cornfield. They see Fred lying on the ground.

"Fred!" Daphne shouts and rushes to his side.

"Fred, what happened?" Velma asks as she and Daphne help him to his feet.

"One of the aliens zapped me with a ray gun, but then it left me here," Fred replies.

"Let's leave before the alien comes back," Velma suggests.

"Where should we go?" Daphne asks.

"We should get back to the Mystery Machine. We'll be safe there," Fred says.

The three friends pause and look at each other.

"Which way is the van?" Velma asks.

Daphne shrugs. Fred scratches his head.

"Oh, great," Velma moans.

Turn the page.

Suddenly it doesn't matter where the Mystery Machine is parked. The aliens burst out of the cornfield on a runaway tractor. The machine heads straight for Daphne, Velma, and Fred. Running in front of the tractor are Shaggy and Scooby!

"*Yaaaa!*" the pals yell as they race past their friends.

Velma, Daphne, and Fred jump out of the way. Shaggy, Scooby, and the aliens circle around inside the clearing and then disappear back into the stalks of corn.

"Since when do aliens know how to drive a farm tractor?" Velma wonders.

"There's a mystery here, and we're going to solve it!" Fred declares. "Follow that tractor!"

"Well, that shouldn't be too hard. It left an obvious trail through the cornfield," Velma observes.

"Then follow that corn!" Fred shouts.

If the trail leads to the saucer, turn to page 73.

If the aliens catch Shaggy and Scooby, turn to page 93.

Shaggy heads back up the ladder in front of the rest of the gang. He climbs up, but he meets someone climbing down. **WHUMP!** Everyone tumbles to the floor. Daphne's flashlight shines on the sheriff.

"Boss! Am I ever glad to see you!" the deputy declares.

"You won't be so glad when I'm finished with you and these meddling kids," the sheriff says.

"Zoinks! The sheriff is an alien!" Shaggy yelps.

"Ruh-roh," Scooby gulps.

"I'm not an alien," the sheriff grumbles. "I told you there was no such thing."

The sheriff presses a hidden button at the bottom of the ladder, and a secret door opens. The gang gasps at what they see on the other side. There is a huge underground aircraft hangar. In the middle of the hangar is the saucer. Gray aliens are everywhere.

"Like, I told you it was an invasion!" Shaggy wails. "We're doomed!"

The sheriff shoves her captives toward the saucer.

"Freddie, what are we going to do?" Daphne asks.

"Don't worry, I have a plan," Fred replies. "Run!"

The gang splits up and runs in different directions. Scooby and Shaggy take off together. The two pals flee through a swinging door and see a sight that makes them stop in their tracks. Cakes and pies and sandwiches and pizzas are stacked on a row of tables. There is a buffet line of pasta and meatballs. A giant pot of mac 'n' cheese bubbles like a gentle golden volcano.

"*Mmmmm*, fooood . . ." Shaggy sighs dreamily.

"*Mmmmm*, rummy . . ." Scooby drools and licks his lips.

All their fears of invasion disappear and are replaced with thoughts of filling their tummies. They pick up serving trays and get in line with the rest of the aliens!

Turn to page 38.

The kids come out from hiding behind the air-conditioning unit on top of a high-rise building. It's night and they can't see what city they're in, but that doesn't interest them right now. They're interested in solving the mystery of the flying saucer! They follow the aliens into the building.

A stairwell leads down to only one door. It's locked, but Daphne takes a nail file from her purse and uses it to work the lock. The door opens into a room that looks like an exhibit hall in a toy museum.

Shaggy is so surprised by what he sees that his arms and legs stick out and his hair stands on end.

"I know where we are!" Shaggy gasps.

"Zackme Toy Company," Velma says. She points to the logo printed on a display case.

"We're in Zackme Toy Headquarters!" Shaggy continues as if he didn't hear Velma. "They make the best toys in the world!"

"Roh boy!" Scooby-Doo says and claps his paws.

Shaggy and Scooby run off to inspect the toys on display. Shaggy finds an exhibit with a flying saucer in it.

"Like, this looks a lot like the saucer we flew in on," Shaggy says. An idea hits him like lightning. "Zoinks! That saucer on the roof is a giant toy!"

"Shaggy, you're right!" Velma says as the rest of the gang gathers around the display case. "You solved the mystery of the saucer!"

"But then, who are the aliens?" Fred wonders.

"Rask rhem?" Scooby gulps and points his paw behind Fred.

The aliens from the saucer stand nearby with ray guns in their hands. The gang can think of only one thing to do.

"Run!" Fred yells.

Turn to page 42.

Scooby-Doo helps Shaggy pull on the tractor's steering wheel. The two of them team up and have enough strength to turn the tractor away from the saucer! The farm machine bounces over the rough furrows and smashes through the cornstalks. Shaggy and Scooby end up with a mouthful of corncobs. The alien is covered from head to toe with cornhusks.

"Shaggy! Scooby! Stop!" Velma yells. She and Daphne come out of the corn rows and run alongside the tractor.

"Like, sure. *How?*" Shaggy yells back.

Suddenly Daphne uses one of her martial arts moves and leaps onto the tractor. She grabs the gearshift and steps on the brakes. **GRRRR-THUNK!** The machine shudders to a halt. The sudden stop makes the alien go flying through the air!

"*Yaaaaaa!*" it yells as it disappears into the corn.

"Zoinks! Like, I didn't know that tractors came with brakes." Shaggy grins. "Nice to know."

"Shaggy! Scooby! I'm so glad you're all right. Where's Fred?" Velma asks.

Shaggy and Scooby look at each other and shrug.

"Re thought he was with rou," Scooby says.

"Uh-oh," Daphne moans. "I hope the aliens didn't get him. We've got to find him!"

"But how?" Shaggy asks.

"We follow the trail," Velma replies. She points to a set of footprints on the ground.

Turn to page 45.

Shaggy and Scooby load up their cafeteria trays with food. They can't resist bowls of mac 'n' cheese, plates of pizza, and, of course, a whole cake. They are so hungry that they don't care that there are aliens all around them. Suddenly the cafeteria doors swing open and the sheriff bursts into the room.

"There you are!" she yells at Shaggy and Scooby.

"Zoinks!" Shaggy yelps. He and Scooby throw their trays in the air and run.

The two friends escape the sheriff by hiding in a storage closet. They are relieved to escape that danger, but now they face another one. The closet is full of aliens!

The pals are ready to faint from fear when Shaggy realizes that the aliens are really work suits hanging on the wall.

"Like, the aliens are fake! They're just humans wearing these weird suits," Shaggy says. "*Hmmm.* That gives me an idea."

A few minutes later Shaggy and Scooby step out of the closet wearing the alien work suits. They stroll into the underground hangar, and no one notices them as they take a close look at the saucer.

"You know, Scoobs, I've been thinking," Shaggy says.

"Ruh-roh," Scooby gulps.

"If the aliens are fake, I bet this saucer is fake, too," Shaggy says.

"Oh, it's real," says the sheriff from behind them. She pulls off the hoods of their alien suits.

"Zoinks!" Shaggy yelps.

"It's too bad you meddling kids discovered my secret," the sheriff declares.

"It's a good thing they did," the deputy says as he comes up from behind the sheriff and clamps handcuffs on her. "I've been trying to find this secret hangar for a long time."

The deputy pulls off the sheriff's mask. Under the mask is a man's face.

Turn the page.

"If it hadn't been for you kids, Dr. La Greed would have gotten away with stealing my flying saucer secrets," the deputy declares. He pulls off his mask to reveal a woman's face.

"Who are you people?" Shaggy asks, confused.

"My name is Kitty Hawke. I own an aviation design company," the deputy reveals. "Dr. La Greed owns a rival company."

"I was going to build Kitty's saucer first and beat the competition," La Greed admits.

"I knew that the sheriff was La Greed in disguise, so I dressed up as a deputy to keep an eye on him," Kitty says. "I even pestered him about UFOs, hoping he'd slip up somehow."

"Like, his secret would have been safe except for that sandwich in the cornfield," Shaggy reminds them. "Scooby-Doo sniffed out the clue!"

The pals slap a high five and cheer: "Scooby-Dooby-Doooo!"

THE END

To follow another path, turn to page 11.

"Like, run for your life, Scoobs! The aliens are after us!" Shaggy shrieks.

The kids of Mystery Inc. split up and run in different directions. One alien decides to take off after Fred and Velma. The other one starts to go after Shaggy and Scooby. Both aliens smack into each other and fall down!

"Who knew that aliens were so clumsy?" Shaggy observes.

"Ruh-roh!" Scooby gulps as the aliens get up and head straight for him and Shaggy.

The two pals flee as fast as their feet can carry them. They zigzag through the toy museum like it is an obstacle course. Suddenly Shaggy sees something that stops him in his tracks!

"Donnie the Dump Truck! I used to have this when I was a kid!" Shaggy shouts when he sees the toy in a display case. He stops running to take a closer look.

Suddenly Shaggy is caught in a net of sticky string. The aliens have caught up with him! Their ray guns are really goo guns!

"Ri'll save rou!" Scooby shouts as he leaps through the air toward his pal.

The aliens shoot their goo at Scooby, but he twists in the air like a kung fu master. The sticky strands miss him! Scooby lands on top of the aliens and knocks them down. The impact knocks off their masks. "Rey, rhey're rakes!" Scooby says.

Shaggy is still wrapped up in the goo net but he hops over to Scooby and looks at the alien imposters.

"Hey, I know this guy!" Shaggy says and points at one of the unmasked men. "He's Zack Zackme. He owns this toy company!"

"He's also my brother, and he tried to steal my saucer!" a new voice declares.

Shaggy and Scooby turn and see the rest of the gang with a man who looks exactly like Zackme.

Turn the page.

"Everybody, meet Mack Mackme," says Velma, "Zack Zackme's twin and the inventor of the Mack-One Flying Saucer. His brother was trying to steal the design and sell it as his own."

"You meddling kids!" Zackme complains. "I could have made millions with that flying saucer design."

"It doesn't belong to you," Mack Mackme declares. "It's mine and you can't have it."

"If only you had agreed to cut me in, I wouldn't have resorted to this," Zackme retorts.

The twins start to argue in a way only two brothers can argue. The gang isn't about to get into the middle of their sibling rivalry.

"I don't have a brother, Scoobs, but I'm sure glad I have you!" Shaggy declares.

"Re, too!" Scooby agrees. The pals slap a high five. "Scooby-Dooby-Doooo!"

THE END

To follow another path, turn to page 11.

"Uh-oh. I don't like where this is going," Shaggy moans. The trail of footprints leads up to the strange saucer.

"Shhh, Shaggy! We have to be quiet if we want to rescue Fred," Velma warns her friend.

"Like, how do we know he's inside the saucer?" Shaggy asks.

"The aliens are too small to leave a trail of size-twelve shoe prints," Velma replies. "Those prints are from Fred's feet!"

The kids sneak up to the saucer and peek inside the open hatch. The saucer is packed with cages filled with alien animals.

"It . . . it's like a zoo," Velma realizes.

"And Fred is part of the exhibit!" Daphne gasps and points to Fred in a cage.

The pals rush up to Fred and try to find a way to open the cage. He is still groggy from the ray gun shock and can barely move his body.

"Bwubba wubba!" Fred mumbles. His mouth is numb and he can hardly speak.

Turn the page.

Fred tries to point at something. Scooby turns and sees an alien holding a key.

"Ranks," Scooby says and takes the key from the alien.

Scooby-Doo unlocks Fred's cage before he realizes who just handed him the key! *"Yaaaa!"* Scooby shrieks.

"Oh! You Earth creatures are so loud!" the alien complains and puts its hands over its ear openings.

"You . . . you speak our language?" Velma asks in surprise.

"Of course. I come to this planet all the time," the alien replies.

"Do . . . do you come here to kidnap people?" Shaggy stammers and looks around at the caged cargo.

"No! I had some saucer trouble and landed to make repairs," the alien explains. "My name is Bwubba Wubba. Pleased to meet you!"

"Why did you put Fred in a cage?" Daphne demands.

"My service robots made a mistake. They thought he was a specimen that escaped," Bwubba explains. "Let me make it up to you. Will you join me for my daily feast?"

Shaggy and Scooby look at each other and gulp. "As long as *we're* not on the menu!" Shaggy shivers.

"Ha! Ha! You humans are so funny! I'm a vegetarian." Bwubba laughs.

Still, Shaggy and Scooby run out of the saucer as fast as they can. Their friends are right behind them! They watch the saucer fly away.

"I can't believe it!" Shaggy exclaims.

"What? That the alien was real?" Velma asks.

"No. I can't believe he made me lose my appetite!" Shaggy says.

THE END

To follow another path, turn to page 11.

"We can't be at a dead end," Velma says. "The secret hatch and this ladder have to lead to *something*."

Even with Daphne's flashlight the gang can't find any trace of a door. They discover something else instead.

"Look! An air-conditioning vent!" Velma says. "Why is there an air-conditioning vent in a dead-end room?"

"Aw, Velma, please don't say *dead*," Shaggy pleads.

"One of us should go and see where it leads," Fred says.

"I'll try," Daphne answers. "But how do I climb up there?"

"I have a plan!" Fred declares. "We can form a human ladder so Daphne can reach the vent."

Shaggy and Scooby-Doo climb onto Fred's shoulders. The deputy stands on top of Scooby, and Velma balances on the deputy. Daphne wonders how stable the wobbly column is!

"There's nowhere to go but up!" Daphne declares. She climbs over her pals and into the air-conditioning vent.

The vent is short, and Daphne can see a light at the other end. She crawls on her hands and knees toward the light. It's a very short distance. When she reaches the end of the vent she is amazed at the sight on the other side.

"It's the flying saucer!" Daphne gasps.

The marvelous machine sits beneath an underground dome.

"So this is where the saucer disappeared to!" Daphne says.

Suddenly Daphne sees her friends walk into the dome and head toward the saucer. She is about to shout hello before she sees they are surrounded by a group of aliens.

"Oh, no! The gang has been captured!" Daphne realizes. "I'm safe because the aliens didn't know I was in this vent."

Turn the page.

Daphne watches her pals and the deputy be taken into the saucer. She is determined to rescue them. Daphne quietly pops open the air-conditioning vent and drops down to the floor inside the dome. She runs as fast as she can toward the saucer.

Daphne peeks inside the spaceship and sees her friends. They are all tied up and sitting on the floor. She sneaks into the saucer and tippy-toes toward her pals and the deputy. Suddenly the door to the saucer closes behind her! The engines start.

"Jeepers! The saucer is about to take off. But where is it going?" Daphne gulps.

The saucer starts to take off.

"Zoinks! We're being abducted by aliens!" Shaggy wails. "Goodbye, Earth!"

"Ro long, Scooby Snacks!" Scooby whimpers.

"Did someone mention a Scooby Snack?" says an alien standing next to them.

"*Yaaa!*" Shaggy shrieks in surprise.

Turn to page 58.

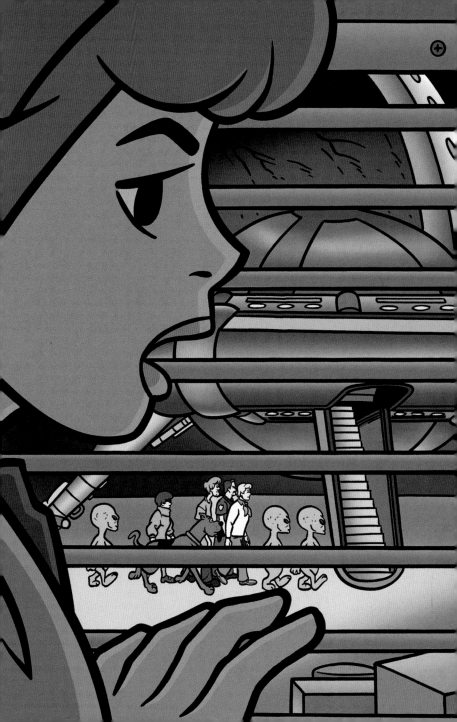

The gang peeks out from behind a large air-conditioning unit on the roof of a high-rise building and watches the aliens exit the saucer. The little gray creatures cover the saucer with a tarp. When they finish, they go into the building.

"Why did they cover the saucer with a tarp? Don't they have, like, an invisibility cloak or something?" Shaggy wonders.

"That's a good question, Shaggy," Velma says. "We should investigate."

"I want to know more about those aliens," Fred declares. "Let's split up."

"Shaggy, Scooby, and I will check out the saucer," Velma suggests.

"Great! Daphne and I will follow the aliens," Fred says.

Fred and Daphne head off across the roof and go into the building. Shaggy and Scooby nervously follow Velma toward the flying saucer.

Velma lifts a section of the tarp and crawls under it.

"Jinkies! It's so dark under here that I can't see anything. It's as bad as losing my glasses," Velma says. "Shaggy! Scooby-Doo! Where are you?"

"Rover rhere," Scooby says.

Velma follows the sound of Scooby's voice until she sees the big, white circles of his eyes. Shaggy blinks beside his pal. There is another small dot of white next to them.

"What's that?" Velma wonders.

"It's not me," Shaggy says.

"Rit's not me, reither," Scooby replies. Then he gulps. "Ruh-roh!"

Velma reaches out and touches the white dot. Brilliant light dazzles their eyes. When their vision adjusts, Velma, Shaggy, and Scooby see the saucer's main hatch open. The stairway folds down.

"I guess I found the door control," Velma concludes. She climbs the stairs and enters the alien saucer.

Turn the page.

Shaggy and Scooby don't really want to go back onboard the scary saucer, but they don't want to let Velma go alone. They follow her into the spaceship and gasp at what they see!

Velma stands in the middle of a round room. There is nothing inside except a control panel on the curved wall, a chair, and lots of TV screens.

"Well, this isn't exactly what I'd call advanced alien technology," Velma declares, disappointed.

"No, this is better!" Shaggy exclaims and rushes to the control panel. "It's a video game!"

Shaggy runs up and down in front of the control panel.

"Like, I've discovered the secret of the saucer. It's a video game!" Shaggy says. "I can't wait to play it!"

"Are you sure you want to play this saucer game, Shaggy? This thing *flew*," Velma warns.

"I'm as sure as my name is Shaggy Rogers!" Shaggy proclaims. "Watch!"

Turn to page 62.

Shaggy and the alien tug on the tractor's steering wheel. Shaggy tries to turn left. The alien tries to turn right. The tractor doesn't turn at all! It heads straight toward the saucer!

"Re're doomed!" Scooby-Doo declares and covers his eyes with his paws.

The alien jumps off the tractor. Shaggy and Scooby get ready for a crash! Suddenly a ramp folds out of the saucer's hull. The tractor zooms up the ramp and disappears into the saucer. The ramp folds up and closes behind Shaggy and Scooby.

The tractor stops all by itself inside the saucer. It's very dark and the two pals can't see anything. Shaggy jumps when he feels something brush up against him.

"Zoinks! S-Scooby-Doo, is that y-you?" Shaggy stammers in fear.

"Ri ron't know," Scooby replies.

"Like, I have a bad feeling about this," Shaggy whimpers.

Turn the page.

The two pals wait to see if their eyes will adjust to the darkness, but nothing happens.

"We can't just sit here, Scoobs. We've got to find a way out," Shaggy says as he climbs down off the tractor. "Which way did we come in?"

"Reats re." Scooby shrugs, even though his friend can't see him.

Shaggy walks through the dark. He stretches out his arms and hands and tries to feel his way. **BONK!** He bumps into something. A dim light turns on.

"Hey, Scooby, I found something!" Shaggy says in relief.

Shaggy looks around and sees that he and Scooby are standing in a large, circular room. Mechanical tubes hang down from the ceiling. The floor has a metal grid marked in it.

"Like, at least we can see where we are, Scooby. But where are we?" Shaggy asks.

The dim light starts to get brighter and brighter. It gets so bright that Shaggy and Scooby can't see anything. The pals try to shield their eyes from the brilliance.

Suddenly they hear a shrill sound. **SHREEEEE!** A final burst of light pops like a camera flash. Shaggy and Scooby blink and try to focus. What they see in front of them makes them shriek. There's something in the room with them that wasn't there before!

"Yaaaa! It's an alien monster!" Shaggy yells.

"Yaaa! Rit's a monster ralien!" Scooby shouts.

Shaggy sees a creature with a dinosaur head and Scooby's body. Scooby sees the head of his pal Shaggy on top of the body of an octopus. The two friends don't realize that they are looking at each other! Something on the saucer has changed them.

"Gronk!" Scooby bellows like a dinosaur. He is very surprised at the sound of his own voice. He could talk just a minute ago!

Turn to page 65.

Shaggy is terrified of the alien standing next to him. His hair stands on end.

"Relax. It's Daphne," Velma says.

"Huh?" Shaggy, Scooby, and Fred gasp.

"It's obvious. The alien is wearing Daphne's purse!" Velma points out.

"Hi!" Daphne says and unzips her alien costume. "Guess what? The aliens are fakes!"

She uses nail clippers from her purse to snip the ropes holding her pals.

"If the aliens are fake, what about this saucer?" Fred wonders.

"It's real, and I'm going to make an arrest for a stolen vehicle," the deputy announces.

The gang follows the deputy to the control room of the flying saucer.

"How did he know where to find the control room?" Velma wonders. "There's more to this mystery than a simple saucer!"

The friends are shocked to see the sheriff flying the spaceship.

"Surrender!" the deputy commands.

The sheriff doesn't obey. She tilts the controls and the saucer tips sideways. Everyone slides along the floor! Scooby-Doo bounces off a wall and flies through the air. He lands on top of the sheriff. She loses control of the saucer and it goes into a dive!

"Ruh-roh," Scooby gulps.

Suddenly the deputy takes control of the saucer. It levels out and flies straight.

"Thanks, kids! If it weren't for you, I would have never found my spaceship," the deputy declares.

"You meddling kids ruined my plan to sell the saucer and its secrets to a foreign government," the sheriff reveals.

"Wait, you're not a deputy. You're a real alien!" Velma realizes.

Turn the page.

"Yes! I used this disguise to get close to the sheriff," the deputy says. He pulls off his mask to reveal a green face and eyestalks. "I hoped she would lead me to my saucer."

"When we reported the crash, she had to make her move," Velma says.

"I almost got away with it, too," the sheriff grumbles.

A while later the saucer lands near the Mystery Machine. Government agents are waiting. They take the sheriff away, but one of the men winks at the gang.

"Thanks for helping my friend find his spaceship," he whispers. He lifts the edge of his mask to reveal green skin.

Mystery Inc. waves goodbye to the saucer as it flies away into the sky. Suddenly the Mystery Machine starts up! The gang climbs into the van and drives toward another adventure.

THE END

To follow another path, turn to page 11.

Shaggy sits down in the command chair. He presses the start button. The video monitors light up. All the lights on the control panel blink and flash. The stairs pull in and the hatch closes.

"Ruh-roh," Scooby gulps.

"Don't worry, Scoobs. It's like a flight simulator," Shaggy says. "We can't pretend to fly if the door is open."

Suddenly the saucer's engines start. They feel the saucer lift into the air.

"Uh, Shaggy, this isn't pretend. We're really taking off!" Velma shouts.

"Warning! Incoming hostiles!" the computer announces. The video screens show a squadron of fighter jets. "Defense systems online."

"Jinkies! It's the Air Force!" Velma yelps. "They think we're a real UFO!"

Suddenly one of the jets fires a missile. The saucer is shaken by the blast. Velma is knocked off her feet. Her glasses fly off her face.

"Oh, great. We're doomed, and I can't even see it," Velma grumbles.

Shaggy grabs a joystick on the control panel and tilts it to the right. The saucer banks to the right. Velma slides along the floor. Her glasses slide out of her reach.

"I don't like this game, Scoobs!" Shaggy shouts.

"Re neither," Scooby agrees as he cowers under the control panel.

"Defense systems standing by," the computer reminds him.

"I'm not going to shoot at the Air Force! They're good guys!" Shaggy protests.

A final blast knocks out all the power on the saucer. They feel themselves drop.

"This is the end! I'm going to miss you, Scooby-Doo!" Shaggy wails.

The saucer lands with a thump and Shaggy falls out of the command chair. Velma bounces across the floor and lands on her glasses.

Turn the page.

"Game over," the computer says. The lights come back on and the hatch opens. "Would you like to play another game?"

Shaggy, Scooby, and Velma do not reply. They run out of the saucer! It is still under the tarp.

"We never moved," Velma gasps in surprise.

They crawl out from under the tarp and see Fred and Daphne. Next to them is a man dressed in part of an alien costume.

"Hi gang! This guy invented the saucer," Fred says. "It's really a video game platform, even though it has separate flying controls!"

"Yeah, we know," Shaggy moans. "We just got a full-scale demo."

"What did you think of the game play?" the inventor asks.

"It was like the real thing," Shaggy replies just before he faints!

THE END

To follow another path, turn to page 11.

Shaggy runs away on eight slimy tentacles. He's used to using legs, so he trips! Shaggy slides across the floor of the space saucer and bumps into some of the strange equipment. **SHREEEEE! FLASH!** The pals are transformed into two new life-forms.

Now Shaggy has an elephant's head and the body of a whale! He is too big for the room. He curls up in the small space and trumpets.

Scooby suddenly has the shape of a seagull and a pony. He flies around the room like a frightened parakeet and hits more of the weird equipment.

SHREEEE! FLASH!

Shaggy looks at himself and sees that he has a tail and four big dog paws.

"Ruh-roh," Shaggy gulps. "Scooby-Doo! I'm you!"

Shaggy looks down at his body. He has Scooby's legs and tail. His hands are shaped like Scooby's paws. He can feel that he has Scooby's long ears and nose.

Turn the page.

"Ris is so cool!" Shaggy says and runs around the room on four canine feet.

BWAM! Shaggy suddenly rams into the nose of a giant beast.

"GRAAAAR!" Scooby roars. He's not Scooby anymore. He is a real alien monster!

"Roinks! Ri have to relp rou, Rooby-Doo!" Shaggy declares. "But how? Rink, Rhaggy, rink!"

Shaggy jumps up at the strange equipment on the ceiling and chomps onto it with Scooby teeth!

SHREEEEE! FLASH! BOOOOM! All the alien equipment in the room shuts down. The chamber goes dark!

"Scooby-Doo, where are you?" Shaggy whispers. He can't see Scooby in the dark.

"Rover rere," Scooby replies.

"Like, are you still an alien monster?" Shaggy worries. He still can't see his friend.

"Rope, are rou?" Scooby-Doo replies.

At last Shaggy spots his pal. They are back to normal! "Scooby-Doo! You're you again!" Shaggy shouts and hugs his friend.

Suddenly the alien from the tractor bursts into the chamber.

"You meddling humans! You ruined my experiment!" the alien complains. "I was recording Earth life-forms and you made the equipment go crazy."

"Like, it was an accident! Sorry," Shaggy says. "But that machine made Scooby and me into monsters!"

"Oh, you weren't real monsters. That was just a hologram program," the alien explains.

Shaggy and Scooby look at each other and grin. They have an idea.

"Cool! Can we do it again?" the pals say together.

THE END

To follow another path, turn to page 11.

The robots chase Daphne, Shaggy, and Scooby into the kitchen. Daphne finds a control panel with rows of buttons. They are labeled in a language none of them recognize.

"Like, how do we know which button does what?" Shaggy asks.

"Re don't!" Scooby answers.

"Just press one and see what happens," Daphne suggests. The robots surround them. "Hurry!"

Shaggy shuts his eyes and pokes a button.

All the cupboard doors pop open. He presses another button. Water gushes out of the sink faucet. The robots close in on Shaggy and his friends.

"Let's all try at once," Daphne says.

The gang hits all the buttons on the panel. Everything in the kitchen activates at the same time. The stove goes on and off. The refrigerator opens and shuts. The robots spin. Suddenly the control panel squeals and sparks.

"Ruh-roh," Scooby gulps.

"Like, I think we made it worse," Shaggy observes. "What do we do now?"

"Run!" Daphne shouts as the robots roll toward her and her friends.

The terrified trio tries to race out of the kitchen. Their legs spin like windmills. Their feet hit the floor running but they don't go anywhere!

Shaggy looks behind him and sees a robot holding him by the back of his shirt. A second robot has Daphne by the hem of her skirt. Another robot grips Scooby's tail.

"Zoinks! The Smart House has outsmarted us!" Shaggy declares.

"Re're doomed!" Scooby whimpers.

Turn to page 75.

Shaggy and Scooby try to flee from the strange gray aliens, but their feet spin on the wet floor. They can't get a grip! A tall spray of water gushes out behind the two pals. The aliens don't have the same problem. They rush toward Shaggy and Scooby.

"Zoinks! We're doomed!" Shaggy cries.

"Ruh-roh!" Scooby gulps as he loses his balance. He tumbles into Shaggy.

Shaggy and Scooby fall onto the slick floor and start to slide. Their legs still spin like boat propellers. Suddenly the pair zooms away on their tummies.

"It's like we're bodysurfing, Scoobs!" Shaggy laughs. "Surf's up!"

"Scooby-Dooby-Doooo!" Scooby howls.

The friends zip across the floor as fast as they can go. They escape the aliens, but they are heading toward the dome at full speed.

"Put on the brakes!" Shaggy shouts.

"What rakes?" Scooby gulps.

Turn the page.

Scooby and Shaggy speed toward the dome and can't stop. They've escaped the aliens but they are in bigger trouble now! They are about to crash through the dome and into the ocean on the other side.

Suddenly the water changes direction under Shaggy and Scooby. It carries them along a new current. They miss hitting the dome.

"Like, that's a relief!" Shaggy sighs, just before he and Scooby are swallowed up by a huge whirlpool!

"*Yaaaaa!*" Shaggy and Scooby yell as they get sucked down the hole. "We're *dooooooomed!*"

Shaggy and Scooby are sucked into the whirlpool like they were flushed down a toilet. They travel down a tube and finally get dumped out into a tank full of water. The pals doggie paddle around but can't find a way out of the tank. Suddenly Shaggy feels something touch his leg.

Turn to page 79.

Fred, Velma, and Daphne follow the trail made by the tractor chasing Scooby and Shaggy. The path twists and turns and loops around! At last it leads them to the flying saucer. The spaceship is sealed up tight.

"Oh, no! Do you think the aliens captured Shaggy and Scooby?" Daphne worries.

"If these tracks in the dirt are any clue, I'd say yes," Velma says and points to large paw marks and big footprints leading up to the saucer.

"They must be inside the saucer!" Daphne exclaims.

"There was an open hatch when we first saw the saucer. Where is it now?" Velma asks.

Fred presses his palms against the hull. He feels around for a seam or a joint. He goes all around the saucer but can't find the way into the ship.

"Shaggy and Scooby are doomed," Daphne sniffs.

Turn the page.

74

Suddenly the hatch into the space ship appears. *WHOOOSH!*

"You did it, Fred!" Velma exclaims.

"Okay, just don't ask me to do it again." Fred laughs nervously. He has no idea why it opened.

The gang enters the saucer. They are happy to see Shaggy and Scooby-Doo! Then they gasp at a surprising sight. There are two Shaggies and two Scoobies!

"Am I seeing double?" Fred wonders and rubs his eyes.

"Jeepers! I see them, too," Daphne stammers.

Shaggy and Scooby . . . and Shaggy and Scooby . . . are strapped to alien exam tables in a lab.

"Relp!" Scooby yells.

"Relp!" the other Scooby shouts.

"Who is the real Scooby-Doo?" Velma asks.

Turn to page 82.

Daphne, Shaggy, and Scooby can't get away from the Smart House robots. The kids are doomed if they don't escape! Daphne searches inside her purse for something to break the grip of the robots.

"Hey, guys! I found a screwdriver!" Daphne shouts to her friends.

Suddenly one of the mechanical menaces grabs her purse and the screwdriver.

"Hey! Give that back! That purse matches my outfit," Daphne protests.

The robot throws Daphne's purse through the kitchen window. **CRASH!** Shaggy and Scooby put their hands and paws to their mouths and gasp.

"You did *not* just *do* that . . ." Shaggy whispers to the robot.

No one in the kitchen moves. All action stops. Shaggy and Scooby wait to see what Daphne will do next. So do the robots!

Turn the page.

"You wrecked my purse," Daphne says in a low voice.

Daphne glares at the robot that did the deed. She points her finger at the machine. "*You. Wrecked. My. Purse!*"

EEEP! The robot squeaks. It turns and runs away from the furious girl. The other robots let go of Shaggy and Scooby and follow their mechanical friend. Daphne stands in the middle of the kitchen with her hands on her hips. The faucet still gushes water and the cupboards continue to open and close. The control panel throws out sparks. Suddenly a short, thin alien runs into the room.

"You broke my house!" he shouts.

The alien pulls the control panel off the wall. Behind it is a big, red button. He hits the button and the entire house shuts off.

"My whole experiment is ruined," the alien moans.

"Experiment?" Shaggy gulps.

"I'm studying human behavior," the small alien says.

The alien presses another button and the house disassembles around them. Fred, Velma, and the deputy stand nearby, surprised.

"The house was an experimental habitat," the alien explains. "It was also my saucer."

The house components come back together to form the flying saucer.

"Now it's broken, too," the alien moans.

"Don't worry, little guy. We'll help you fix it," Fred says.

"You will?" the alien asks.

"Sure!" Daphne says as she picks up her purse and screwdriver.

"Thank you. Humans aren't so bad, after all," the alien smiles.

THE END

To follow another path, turn to page 11.

"Uh, Scoobs. Was that you?" Shaggy gulps.

"Rope," Scooby replies.

The "something" grabs Shaggy's leg and pulls him under the water. He looks into alien eyeballs!

"*Yaaaa!*" Shaggy shrieks.

"*Eeee!*" a shrill voice replies.

Shaggy and Scooby try to escape from the tank, but there is no way out. They can't even find the way they came in! Suddenly they feel hundreds of tentacles wrap around their bodies.

"I don't know what's in this tank, but it's going to be the last thing we ever see!" Shaggy wails.

"Re're roomed!" Scooby whimpers.

It takes him a moment, but Shaggy realizes that the creatures aren't trying to hurt him. They're trying to *hug* him!

"Hey, Scooby, these little guys are nice!" Shaggy says. He pats one on the head and it vibrates like a purring kitty.

Turn the page.

"Rello," Scooby says to a little creature hanging onto his collar.

"RAAAAAR!" a giant creature roars as it bursts up out of the water.

"*Yaaaaa!*" Shaggy and Scooby scream.

The little creatures shriek and flee, except for the one hanging on Scooby's collar. Its tentacle is stuck! The big alien creature grabs Scooby with a giant tentacle and lifts him out of the tank. It stares at Scooby with angry alien eyes.

"Ruh-roh," Scooby gulps.

Suddenly all of the small creatures get between Scooby and the big alien. They wave their tentacles and make noises that sound like chirping. The giant creature blinks its enormous eyes and drops Scooby in the water.

Suddenly Fred, Velma, and Daphne slide down a chute and land in the water with Shaggy and Scooby. One of the gray aliens is right behind them. Shaggy is surprised to see the humanoid alien change into a creature with tentacles.

"Don't worry, the aliens are friendly! These language disks let us talk to each other," Velma says and points to a silver disk on her forehead.

The alien puts disks on Shaggy and Scooby.

"Hello! We're exploring your planet's oceans. Um, why are you in the day-care center?" the alien asks.

"Like, we made a wrong turn?" Shaggy says.

"Oh! I thought you were scaring the children. Sorry," the giant creature says and shrugs its tentacles. "I'm the nanny."

"Can we play with the aliens?" a little alien asks.

"Okay, but be gentle. They're fragile beings and might break," the enormous nanny replies.

Shaggy and Scooby get swamped by their new friends.

"Scooby-Dooby-Dooooo!" Scooby whoops.

THE END

To follow another path, turn to page II.

There are two Shaggy Rogers and a pair of Scoobies inside the alien saucer. Fred, Velma, and Daphne are astonished at this amazing sight!

"Who's who?" Daphne wonders.

"Ri'm the real Scooby-Doo," one Scooby says.

"Ruh-ruh! Ri'm the rone and ronly!" the other Scooby declares.

The twin canines glare at each other even strapped down on the exam tables.

"Get me out of here! Those guys are clones!" one Shaggy says.

"No way! Like, that guy's a fake!" the other Shaggy replies. "What are we going to do? We can't free the clones," Daphne worries.

"Worse than that, how can we tell that they're telling the truth?" Fred says. "All four of them could be aliens!"

"You're right, Fred! The aliens could be disguised as Shaggy and Scooby!" Velma says. "I know one way to find out."

Velma stomps over to one of the Shaggies. She stares him in the eyes and then grabs a clump of his hair. She pulls!

"Zoinks!" Shaggy yelps.

"*Hmmm*," Velma mutters.

She marches over to the other Shaggy and pulls on his hair, too.

"Ow!" Shaggy yells.

"Double *hmmm*," Velma says. "I've concluded that neither Shaggy is an alien in disguise. They're not wearing masks."

"We're clones, not aliens," Shaggy grumbles.

Velma turns toward the two Scoobies. They cower and tremble.

"I have a better idea," Velma grins. "Daphne, give me your purse. I know how to tell who's the real Scooby-Doo."

Velma takes Daphne's purse and pulls out a box of treats.

"Who wants a Scooby Snack?" Velma asks.

Turn the page.

Scooby-Doo breaks free of the straps holding him as if they were made of wet spaghetti. The other Scooby doesn't move a muscle. The real Shaggy Rogers leaps off the exam table, too! He gobbles down a Scooby Snack.

"Mmmm! Rummy!" the real Scooby-Doo says.

"Like, there's nothing in this world like a Scooby Snack!" the real Shaggy declares.

Suddenly a gray alien stomps up to Mystery Inc.

"You meddling kids! You wrecked my experiment!" the alien complains. "I was creating clones to take over your planet!"

"And you could have done it, too, if you hadn't tried to clone me and Scooby-Doo!" Shaggy proclaims.

Shaggy and Scooby slap a high five.

"Scooby-Dooby-Dooooo!" they shout!

THE END

To follow another path, turn to page 11.

Fred and the deputy fight off the menacing robots as Velma studies the computer screen on the wall of the Smart House.

"It seems like a simple touch screen," Velma says. She places a finger on the blank surface of the monitor. The screen lights up.

"Get it to turn off the house, or at least stop these robots!" Fred shouts.

"Well, I can't just hit a command at random! It might make things worse," Velma says reasonably.

"Believe me, it can't get much worse," the deputy declares as one of the machines grabs him with a metal claw. The robot shakes him like a rattle.

Velma glances at her friends and sees them in trouble. She doesn't like to make a rushed decision, but this time she doesn't have a choice. Velma touches a random symbol on the computer screen.

Suddenly the robots stop attacking her friends. The machines back off and stand a few feet away from Fred, Velma, and the deputy.

"You did it, Velma!" Fred says.

"You're a genius!" the deputy praises her.

"I was lucky." Velma sighs with relief. "Let's find the rest of the gang and get out of here."

"Um, Velma, why are the robots glowing?" Fred wonders. The machines blaze with a very bright light. The light intensifies and finally explodes in a brilliant burst.

At first Fred, Velma, and the deputy can't see. When their sight recovers they can't believe their eyes!

They are standing in the middle of an alien landscape. The ground is barren and looks like dried mud. The sky is purple. There are mountains in the distance that look like the rounded humps of the Loch Ness monster.

"I don't think we're in Kansas anymore," Fred gasps.

Turn the page.

"I don't think we're even on Earth!" the deputy declares.

They hear the roar of a tremendous beast. The ground shakes and then splits open. Giant creatures climb up out of the chasm.

"Nope! We're not on Earth!" Fred agrees.

"But . . . how did we get here?" Velma shouts over the howls of the beasts.

"Maybe that saucer you saw had something to do with it," the deputy says.

"How?" Velma asks.

"Maybe it teleported us here. I don't know! You're the genius!" the deputy replies.

"Right now it doesn't matter *how* we got here. Right now we've got to get *out* of here!" Fred declares. "Run!"

Turn to page 96.

"Eww! What's on this floor?" Daphne says as she and Velma try to run away from the aliens.

"I told you. It's just water," Velma replies.

"Does that mean the dome is leaking?!" Daphne worries.

"Um, I didn't think about that," Velma admits.

"Quick! We can hide in there!" Daphne says and points to a warehouse.

They run inside and see a room filled with packing crates. Daphne and Velma jump inside the nearest crate and hide. They think they're safe until a forklift grabs the crate!

Daphne reaches into her purse and pulls out a flashlight. She turns it on and gasps. Glittering gold sparkles in front of her eyes!

"Oh! It's beautiful!" Daphne sighs.

"But why is it here in an underwater dome?" Velma wonders.

"It's a mystery and we're going to solve it!" Daphne declares.

Turn the page.

Daphne and Velma stay inside the crate until it is put down. They wait a few minutes and then peek out to see where they are.

"Oh, no! We're back inside the saucer!" Velma observes.

"Velma? Is that you?" Shaggy says. He and Scooby-Doo poke their heads out of a nearby crate.

"Hi, gang!" Fred says and pops out of another crate. "I guess the plan to split up didn't work!"

"Like, there's a bunch of gold and stuff in here," Shaggy says as he climbs out of his crate.

"In here, too," Fred says.

"Same here," Daphne says as she and Velma crawl out of their crate.

"These guys are stealing our Earth treasures!" Shaggy declares. "The aliens are art thieves!"

Suddenly Scooby and the gang feel the saucer start to lift off.

"Zoinks! We're launching into outer space!" Shaggy panics.

"Come on, gang. We're not going to let these aliens take our Earth treasures into outer space!" Fred declares as he jumps out of his crate.

"Like, how are we going to stop them?" Shaggy wonders.

Fred points to a map on the wall that shows the layout of the saucer.

"We get to the control room and take over the spaceship!" Fred says.

"Roh reah!" Scooby-Doo declares.

It doesn't take long for the kids to get to the saucer's control room. They burst in and take the alien pilot by surprise. Fred pulls the alien from the control seat and Scooby sits on him. Fred takes over the controls, but . . .

"Um, I don't know how to fly this thing," Fred gulps.

The saucer swerves and weaves inside the underwater dome. Suddenly the saucer hits the dome. *CRAAAACK!*

"Ruh-roh!" Scooby gulps.

Turn to page 99.

Fred, Velma, and Daphne chase after the tractor that is chasing Shaggy and Scooby-Doo. The trail isn't straight, but it is easy to follow. The gang zigzags all over the cornfield until they finally find the tractor. Shaggy and Scooby are nowhere in sight. Neither are the aliens.

"Oh, no! Do you think Shaggy and Scooby were abducted by aliens?" Daphne worries.

"Scooby-Doo! Where are you?" Velma shouts.

There is no answer. The only thing the gang hears is the sound of the wind blowing through the cornstalks. Shaggy and Scooby can't hear their friends call out. They are inside the saucer and heading into outer space!

"Like, we've been abducted by aliens!" Shaggy moans. He and Scooby are strapped to exam tables in an alien lab.

A gray alien puts sticky sensors on Shaggy's forehead. The sensors are connected to a strange machine. The alien turns it on.

Turn the page.

As soon as the alien turns on the machine, suddenly Shaggy isn't on the flying saucer anymore. He's in a forest. It's dark and scary. It's also familiar!

"Hey, I've been here before," Shaggy realizes. "This is where Scooby and I saw . . ."

ROAAAR! A big, hairy beast stomps out of the forest and heads straight for Shaggy.

"Oh, yeah. We saw Bigfoot! Zoinks!" Shaggy shrieks. He runs through the woods as fast as he can. Shaggy doesn't know where he's going until he reaches a cave. He rushes inside to hide.

"Whew! I never thought I'd see that Bigfoot beast again," Shaggy says and gasps for breath.

He thinks he's safe until he realizes there's something in the cave with him. A slimy tentacle flops at his feet. Shaggy turns around to see a creature that looks like a giant octopus.

"*Yaaa!* A sea creature!" Shaggy shouts in alarm.

Shaggy doesn't stop to wonder what a sea creature is doing in a cave in the woods. He runs! Shaggy races deeper into the cave until he reaches an underground temple. This looks familiar, too.

"Like, this is the Aztec tomb we found in Mexico," Shaggy realizes. "How did I get here?"

The answer to that question doesn't really matter, because Shaggy sees a pack of chupacabras running toward him. Leading them is a dog-headed Aztec warrior. Shaggy recognizes the menacing monster.

"Xolotl! The Aztec god of the dead!" Shaggy gulps. "I'm doomed!"

Turn to page 103.

Fred, Velma, and the deputy run across an alien landscape. They don't know how they got here. They don't have time to think about that. Giant creatures come up out of the ground and chase them!

Velma runs as fast as she can. Suddenly she stubs her toe on a rock. She falls down and her glasses go flying off her face. The breath is knocked out of her lungs. She can't call out to her fleeing friends for help! They keep running, never knowing that she has fallen. Without her glasses, she can't see them anyway.

I am so doomed! Velma thinks as a giant, blurry shape looms over her.

"Allow me to assist you, fair lady!" a voice says. A human hand grips Velma's wrist and pulls her to her feet.

"Fred?" Velma wonders.

The blurry shape gives Velma her glasses. She puts them on and sees a knight in shining armor and a helmet stands in front of her.

"You're not Fred," Velma realizes.

"I'm your hero, and I'm here to rescue you!" the knight declares.

One of the giant alien creatures rears up to attack the knight, but he uses a glowing sword to defeat it. **FWOOOSH!** The monster disappears in a burst of light. Another creature comes up out of the ground! It chomps down on the knight with giant jaws! **FWOOOOSH!** The beast disappears just like the other one.

"Ta-da!" the knight says and bows toward Velma.

"Look out behind you!" Velma warns and points to something behind the knight.

He turns to look. Nothing is there. **CLAAAANG!** Velma uses an alien rock to knock out the knight!

"You're a fake," Velma declares.

Velma grabs the knight's helmet to pull it off his head. As soon as she touches the helmet, the alien landscape disappears. She is back in the Smart House!

Turn the page.

Fred and the rest of the gang sit on the floor looking very confused. Velma is not confused. She knows who is behind this mystery!

"Gibby Norton!" Velma declares.

"Hi, Velma!" Gibby grins as he removes his hologram helmet. "How did you like my game?"

"It wasn't very convincing. I knew it was a fake the minute I saw a medieval knight on an alien planet. I mean, get real!" Velma scoffs.

"I'll do better next time," Gibby promises. "And I won't stop trying until I finally impress you!"

"Who is Gibby Norton?" the deputy whispers to Fred.

"Computer genius, in love with Velma. Long story," Fred whispers back.

"Aw, why couldn't it have been aliens?" the deputy sighs.

THE END

To follow another path, turn to page 11.

Fred tries to fly the saucer but it rams into the underwater dome. **_CRUUNCH!_**

"Yikes! This isn't the same as driving the Mystery Machine!" Fred gulps.

Suddenly the ocean starts to gush in through the cracked dome. Humans and gray aliens run out of the warehouse building. Velma wiggles her glasses to get a good look at them.

"Hey! Those aren't aliens, they're humans in gray wet suits!" Velma declares.

"That means this alien pilot isn't from outer space at all!" Daphne declares. She pulls off his mask and reveals a human face. "He's a fake!"

Suddenly a huge wave of water bursts through the dome. The saucer gets caught up in the surge and is carried away like a twig in a river. The Mystery Inc. gang tumbles head over heels inside the saucer.

"_Yaaaaa!_" they yell.

Turn to page 101.

"Zoinks! We're doomed!" Shaggy wails. He holds on to Scooby as tight as he can. So does the fake alien!

The saucer gets washed out of the underwater dome and floats to the surface of the ocean.

"Hey, that wasn't so bad, Scoobs," Shaggy sighs.

"I'm not sure about that," Fred warns.

All the fake aliens from the underwater dome come up to the surface and climb onto the floating saucer like it's a lifeboat, but their weight starts to make it sink!

"Ruh-roh," Scooby says.

"Ahoy, alien vessel!" a booming voice declares.

"I recognize that voice! It's my cousin, Coast Guard Captain Robert Dinkley!" Velma cheers. She presses a speaker button on the control panel. "Ahoy, Captain Dinkley! This is Velma!"

Turn the page.

"Velma? What are you doing on a secret smuggling saucer?" Captain Dinkley says.

"Come aboard, cousin, and we'll tell you all about it!" Velma declares.

A few minutes later Velma and her cousin meet as the Coast Guard arrests the fake aliens.

"We would have gotten away with our art-theft operation if it hadn't been for you meddling kids!" the fake alien pilot declares. "The flying saucer was the perfect distraction. Too bad it had engine trouble in Kansas."

"I'm glad we figured out the secret of the flying saucer," Velma says. "There's only one more mystery we have to solve."

"What?" Fred asks.

"How do we get back to the Mystery Machine in Kansas?!" Velma says.

THE END

To follow another path, turn to page 11.

Shaggy is more confused than normal. At first he is on a flying saucer. The next thing he knows he is being chased by Bigfoot. Now he's in an underground cave being chased by Xolotl. But Shaggy doesn't have time to wonder about that. All he can think about is running!

Shaggy takes off on spinning legs. He doesn't look where he's going and falls into a hole in the ground. He falls and falls and falls.

"Zoinks! I've fallen into a bottomless pit and I can't get out," Shaggy moans.

At last he lands with a *THUMP!* Shaggy looks around and realizes he's not in a cave anymore. He's inside a house. It has old-fashioned furniture and a portrait hanging on the wall. The portrait is very familiar. Suddenly its eyes move!

"*Yaaa!* I'm back in the house on Spooky Street!" Shaggy wails. "Ghosts and witches and vampires live here!"

Turn the page.

As soon as Shaggy says those words, a ghost, a witch, and a vampire appear. His greatest fears surround him! There is only one thing that can save him.

"Scooby-Doo! Where are you?" Shaggy yells.

Suddenly the great brown canine bursts through the wall of the house on Spooky Street!

"Scooby-Dooby-Doooo!" Scooby shouts. He braces himself on his hind legs and strikes a kung fu pose. The ghost, witch, and vampire look at each other and disappear. *POOF!*

"Scooby! You're the greatest pal ever!" Shaggy declares and hugs his friend.

Suddenly the house on Spooky Street fades away around Shaggy and Scooby. They are back in the flying saucer! A gray alien takes off the sticky sensors from Shaggy's forehead.

"Thank you for your memories. They were very unusual!" a gray alien says.

Shaggy is released from the exam table. The gray alien shakes Shaggy's hand.

"Wonderful!" the alien declares. "You've encountered ghosts, vampires, and sea monsters on the same planet! You're the greatest!"

"Like, it's the first time I've been called that!" Shaggy says. "Um, can I go home now?"

"Sure, but remember — *you were never here,*" the alien replies. "You were *never* here . . ."

Suddenly Shaggy wakes up in the back of the Mystery Machine! The gang is driving down a country road in Kansas. Scooby-Doo snoozes next to him holding an empty box of Scooby Snacks. It's as if nothing ever happened.

"Zoinks! I just had the craziest dream that I was abducted by aliens!" Shaggy declares.

"Well, it's no wonder! You ate a whole box of Scooby Snacks. It must have given you nightmares!" Daphne laughs.

THE END

To follow another path, turn to page 11.

AUTHOR

Laurie S. Sutton has read comics since she was a kid. She grew up to become an editor for Marvel, DC Comics, Starblaze, and Tekno Comics. She has written Adam Strange for DC, Star Trek: Voyager for Marvel, plus Star Trek: Deep Space Nine and Witch Hunter for Malibu Comics. There are long boxes of comics in her closet where there should be clothing and shoes. Laurie has lived all over the world. She currently resides in Florida.

ILLUSTRATOR

Scott Neely has been a professional illustrator and designer for many years. Since 1999, he's been an official Scooby-Doo and Cartoon Network artist, working on such licensed properties as Dexter's Laboratory, Johnny Bravo, Courage the Cowardly Dog, Powerpuff Girls, and more. He has also worked on Pokémon, Mickey Mouse Clubhouse, My Friends Tigger & Pooh, Handy Manny, Strawberry Shortcake, Bratz, and many other popular characters. He lives in a suburb of Philadelphia and has a scrappy Yorkshire Terrier, Alfie.

GLOSSARY

abducted (ab-**DUKT**-ed)—carried a person away using force; kidnapped

aviation (ay-vee-**AY**-shuhn)—the science of building and flying planes and other aircrafts

chupacabra (choo-pah-**CAH**-bruh)—an animal from Mexican legends that is believed to drink the blood of goats

GPS (**JEE PEE ES**)—short for Global Positioning System; a radio system that uses signals from satellites to tell you where you are and how to get to other places

hangar (**HANG**-ur)—a large building where planes and other aircraft are kept

hatch (**HACH**)—a small door or opening on the outside of an aircraft

hull (**HUHL**)—the outer frame of a ship, airplane, or spaceship

invasion (in-**VAY**-zhuhn)—the act of an army or large force coming into an area to take over

landing strut (**LAN**-ding **STRUHT**)—a metal support bar that helps an aircraft land on the ground

specimen (**SPESS**-uh-muhn)—something that is collected as an example of a certain kind of thing, or something that is used for testing and examining

YOU CHOOSE JOKES!

YOU CHOOSE which punch line is funniest!

Why did the scientist throw his dishes out the window?

a. He wanted to see a flying saucer.

b. He was hungry, and it was time for "launch."

c. He thought empty cups had no gravi-tea!

Why did the aliens walk out of the restaurant on the moon?

a. The moon was full.

b. It's boring — there's no atmosphere.

c. They'd have to be lunar-tics to stay there!

What did the alien say to the gas pump?

a. "It's rude to stick your finger in your ear when I'm talking to you!"

b. "You must be a terrific cook. Everyone leaves here full!"

c. "You sure have a fuel-ish look on your face!"

What does Scooby have when he's hungry in outer space?

a. **Mars bars.**
b. **A shake from the Milky Way.**
c. **An asteroid sandwich; it's "meteor" than a regular sandwich.**

Why did Shaggy think there were aliens in his kitchen cupboards?

a. **He saw an Unidentified Frying Object!**
b. **He heard that an extraterrestrial was really "eat-y!"**
c. **He thought they were looking for outer spice!**

What did the little alien get for his birthday?

a. **A bunch of comet books!**
b. **A bag of Martian-mallows!**
c. **Nothing, because no one had the time to "planet!"**

Who was the first animal in outer space?

a. **Pluto**
b. **The cow that jumped over the moon!**
c. **A cat that said, "Take me to your litter!"**

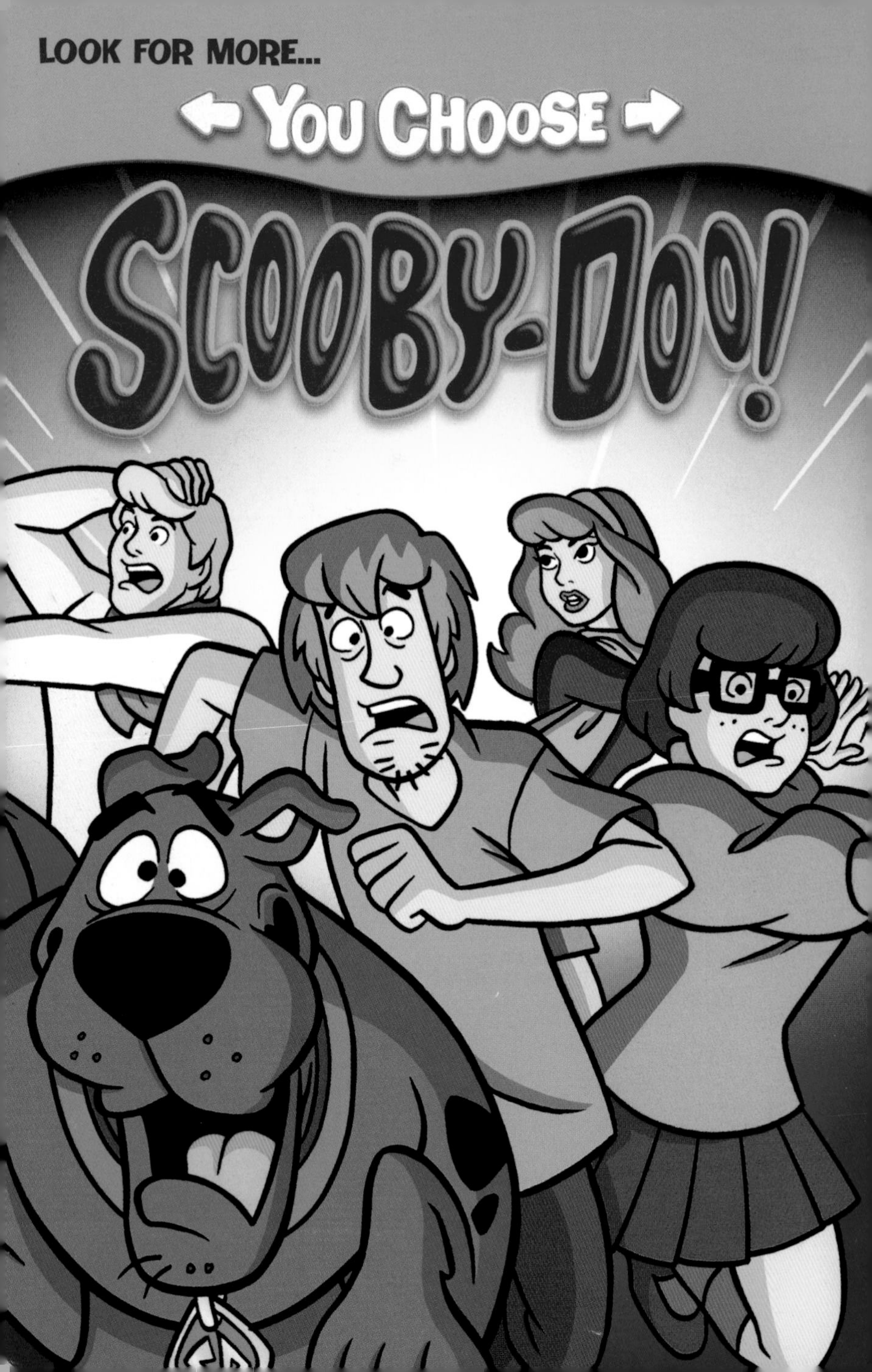
LOOK FOR MORE...
YOU CHOOSE
SCOOBY-DOO!

THE CHOICE IS YOURS!

THE **FUN** DOESN'T STOP HERE!

DISCOVER MORE AT...

www.CAPSTONEKIDS.com